For my daughter, Celeste, and her "giant," my husband, Tom.

First published in the United States of America in 2003 by
Walker Publishing Company, Inc.

Published simultaneously in Canada by Fitzhenry and Whiteside, Markham, Ontario L3R 4T8

For information about permission to reproduce selections from
this book, write to Permissions, Walker & Company, 435 Hudson Street, New York, New York 10014

Library of Congress Cataloging-in-Publication Data

Ewart, Claire.
The giant / Claire Ewart.
p. cm.
Summary: As the seasons pass on the family farm after her mother's death, a young girl
searches for the giant that her mother said would look after her.
ISBN 0-8027-8835-1 — ISBN 0-8027-8837-8 (reinforced)
[1. Grief—Fiction. 2. Fathers and daughters—Fiction. 3. Farm life—Fiction. 4.
Seasons—Fiction.] I. Title.

PZ7.E947 Gi 2002
[E]—dc21
2002028070

The artist used watercolor on 100 percent rag hot press watercolor paper to create the illustrations for this book.

Book design by Victoria Allen

Visit Walker & Company's Web site at www.walkerbooks.com

Printed in Hong Kong

2 4 6 8 10 9 7 5 3 1

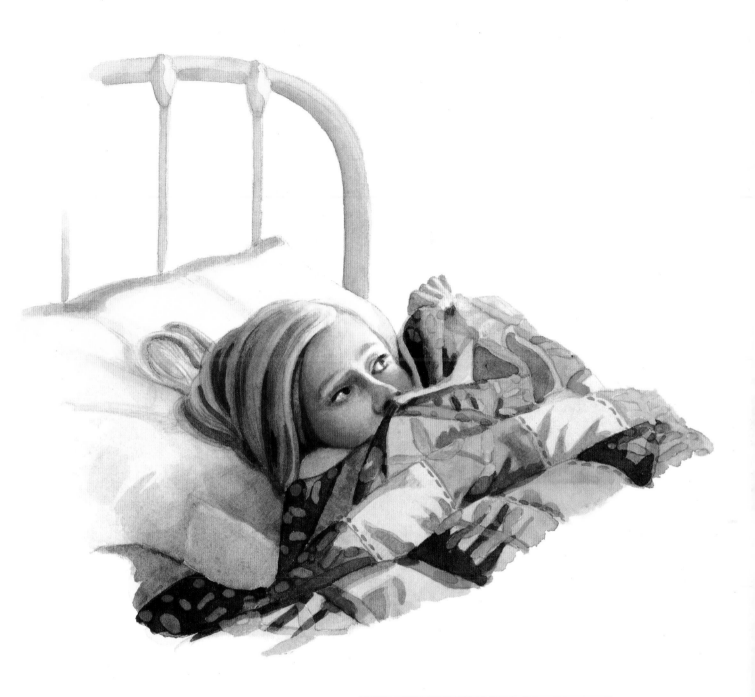

Early one morning,
the clouds rumbled with thunder.
I smelled rain coming
and scrunched under the covers,
missing Mama something awful.

Pa's voice boomed up the stairs,
"Planting time is soon.
Plenty of chores to do."
I pulled on my sweater,
wishing for warmer words.

Outside, the wet wind howled.
Small lakes formed
where ponds and low spots had been,
like Pa's big boot prints,
like huge feet had walked across the land.
And geese came there to nest.

I wondered about
the rumble, and those footprints . . .
Had a giant thundered past?
I remembered
Mama had said there were giants,
strong and tall,
and that one was looking after me.
I needed to see one,
to believe.

Days went by,
and when the fields dried,
Pa strode out,
his shadow stretching
over rumpled grasses.
He checked the dirt
and hitched the horses.
"Lot to get done," he said.

I helped him plow
the wind-flattened land.
Horses breathing,
heavy clods heaving.
And I asked about Mama's giant.
Pa squinted, slapped the reins,
and said, "There's no such thing."
But, I crooked my neck,
searching the thunderheads.
There had to be
a giant who'd look after me.

Spring days warmed the land.
Soon pale lime shoots
nudged up through the soft soil.
Downy goslings scooted after water bugs.
Each day while I did my chores,
I searched for signs of the giant.
Each evening when the sun sank low,
my eyes half closed, I milked the cow,
who made chewing sounds,
as *swish, swish,* milk sprayed into the bucket.
Chickens clucked and muttered in the rafters,
as I listened for the giant.

One evening, when the milk pail was full,
the moon hung in the sky like a lantern.
I climbed to the hayloft,
aching to see
great hands out there, somewhere,
stitching the stars to the sky,
writing a message to me.
But all I saw was darkness,
and Pa below, bending over his work,
his own large hands mending a harness.
In the dark it was hard to see,
but I think Pa looked up and smiled at me.

Summer weeks followed.
Redwing blackbirds sang
and cattails grew around the ponds.
Pretty soon, the goslings flew.
Every day, I wished that I could fly too,
to go and find the giant.

Then one warm day when the crops had grown,
dry wind swept the fields
like enormous hands smoothing sheets.
And I heard whispering like Mama's soft voice.
I ran, chasing the waves through the whipping field,
sure this time I'd catch the giant.
But the hands swept away,
and the whispering moved on,
leaving me behind in the dust and heat,
with chores still to be done.
Out of breath, I stumbled to the barn.
Pa was brushing horses,
smoothing his hands along their backs.
"Got to bring the crops in soon," he said.
I looked back at the fields stretching to the sky.
Pa rubbed my head and said, "You're taller than the hay."
Then he stooped and shouldered a sack of feed.

I still wasn't tall enough to find the giant.

Each hot day,
Pa kept working,
back bending,
brow sweating,
chopping, setting,
fixing, mending.
I did my chores,
but I kept looking.

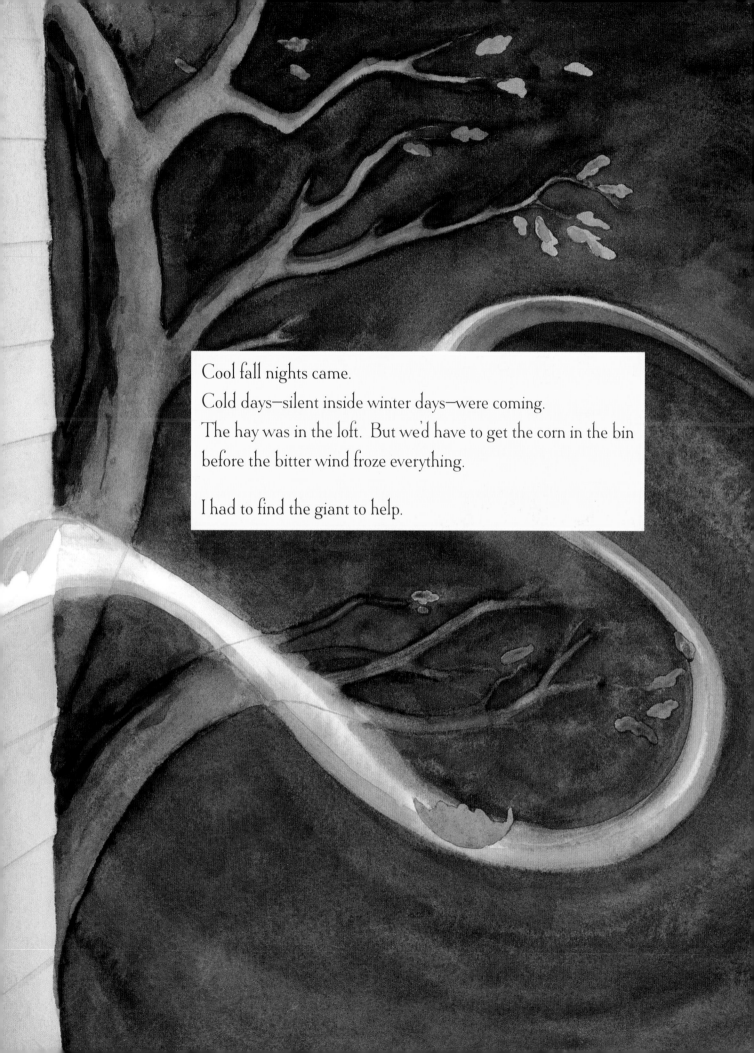

Cool fall nights came.

Cold days—silent inside winter days—were coming.

The hay was in the loft. But we'd have to get the corn in the bin before the bitter wind froze everything.

I had to find the giant to help.

When stalks were crumble-stiff,
and the grown geese honking,
Pa scanned the dark horizon where clouds were looming.
"Time to bring in the corn," Pa called. "Wet weather's comin'."
Thud, thud against the bang board and into the wagon
went ear after hard golden ear.
I shivered as I held the reins,
wanting to gallop the horses to find the giant.
But Pa never stopped as he hooked the corn,
and husked, and swung.
I looked at the rows of corn that stretched on, and on.
I couldn't see how we'd ever get done.

By afternoon lead clouds pulled veils of water
over the low land along the river.
"Bottomland will be turned to muck," said Pa.
We'd never get the corn in if the horses got stuck.
I searched the hills for the giant.

Then, just for a moment, rays of light shot down from the clouds,
like a great brush painting each tree from above.
The trees glowed bright with colors that Mama would have loved.
"Look Pa!" I said, standing high on the wagon seat.
I strained to see the giant coloring each leaf.
But the horses whinnied and reared,
and the wagon lurched away from Pa.

"Hold the horses!" Pa yelled.

His long legs pumped toward us up the slope.

My fingers gripped the reins, but I couldn't hold on.

The wagon tilted, and I stumbled from the seat.

The ears tumbled, nearly knocked Pa down,

but his big arms caught me just before I hit the ground.

"The corn!" I cried. Looking at the mess,
and cold from the rain falling,
I choked, "I'm sorry, Pa."
I don't know how, but the wagon was righted.
The corn was spilled, though, and the giant was gone.
And everything was getting soaked.

Pa rubbed his back, but he didn't complain.
He just set me on the wagon again,
wrapped his coat about my shoulders,
and rubbed me warm.
He looked at me like he was studying something,
then went on working in the rain,
strong as ever,
bringing in the corn.

That day and days after,
coaxing the horses through the mire,
I held the reins till my hands were numb.
I don't know how,
but I kept the horses moving while Pa husked corn.

And one morning when the corn was finally in,
I woke sore on the outside, hurting inside too,
because there was always more to do,
because I stopped believing I'd ever find the giant.
And I missed Mama more than ever,
now that everything was quiet.

That's when I heard the geese gathering,
like far-off dogs yelping.
I ran, remembering
when Mama had woken us
with the whisper, "Let's go see!"

Now, there among the stubble
must have been a hundred geese clustered.
Snow was spitting from the clouds.
Suddenly all at once came the thunder
of wings beating. Like a curtain lifting,
the geese were leaving.

And there was Pa . . . like he'd always been,
standing there, tall and strong in the wind.

My cold fingers found Pa's hard grasp,
his big hands that caught me when I fell,
that rubbed me warm,
that kept on working in the rain,
that brought in the corn.
Together we watched the geese climb
to form a distant V.

Then, his eyes misty,
his hand steadied on my shoulder,
Pa spoke. "I remember how your Mama
loved to watch 'em.
You love 'em too, my girl?"
Pa smiled and touched my chin
with his rugged thumb.
I nodded but couldn't speak.
"My tough girl." Pa sighed and smiled again.
"How you've grown."
A tear ran down my cheek.
I hugged those words,
those warm words, hugging Pa.
Until strong and tall Pa was all I could see.

Now, wrapped snug in the quilt,
I listen as Pa reads,
his tired voice soft,
his rough fingers gentle as he turns the page.

Now I know
what Mama said I'd know.
A giant is looking after me.